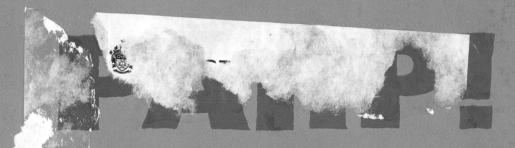

Collect all the Preston Pig Stories

Colin McNaughton
Suddenly!

Colin McNaughton
GOAL!

Colin McNaughton
BOO!

Colin McNaughton
Shh!
(Don't Tell Mister Wolf)
A Preston Pig Lift-the-Flap Book

Colin McNaughton
Oops!

Colin McNaughton
Hmm...
A Preston Pig Story

Colin McNaughton
Oomph!
A Preston Pig Story
Coming soon!

First published in Great Britain by HarperCollins Publishers in 2001

1 3 5 7 9 10 8 6 4 2

ISBN: 0 00 712372 8

From the television series based on the original Preston Pig books created, written and illustrated by Colin McNaughton

Text © Colin McNaughton/HarperCollins Publishers Ltd 2001

Illustrations in this work derived from the television series © Colin McNaughton/Varga-London Ltd 1999

Production of the television series by Varga-London Ltd and Link Entertainment; Licensed by Link Licensing Ltd

The author/illustrator asserts the moral right to be identified as the author/illustrator of the work.

A CIP catalogue record for this title is available from the British Library.

The HarperCollins website address is: www.fireandwater.com

Printed in Hong Kong

Colin McNaughton
PARP!

Collins

An imprint of HarperCollinsPublishers

Ding-a-ling! Ding-a-ling!

School's out. The school piglets skip home.

"Don't forget your music practice tonight," says Miss Thump, the schoolteacher.

Mister Wolf is lurking nearby and he's got bacon on the brain! "Mmm…school dinners. Yum, yum!" says Mister Wolf.

"Now, Preston," says Miss Thump. "I have
to rush. Choose a musical instrument to take
home, then lock up the school. Remember,
I'm leaving you in charge."

"Yes, Miss Thump," says Preston.

In the music room Preston finds a trombone.

Mister Wolf creeps up to the window.

Parp!

"Ow!" says
Mister Wolf.
"That hurt!"

"Fantastic!" says Preston. "What should I try next?"

He tries a violin…**SCREEEECH!**…then a big bass drum…**BOOM BOOM!**

"Phew! This is tiring," says Preston. "I think I'll go and explore."

When Preston has gone Mister Wolf leaps in through the open window…

Preston goes behind
the stage in the
assembly hall.
Mister Wolf creeps
up behind him.

"I wonder what'll happen if I pull this?" says Preston.

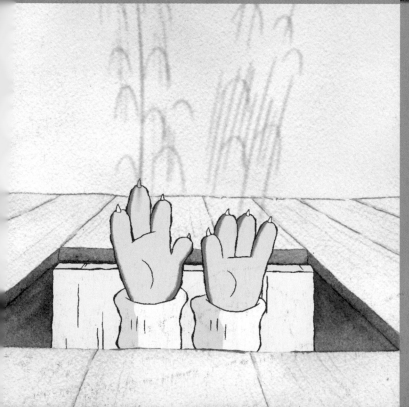

Suddenly Mister Wolf drops through the trap door.

Whee!

"Ow! That hurt," says Mister Wolf.

Preston pushes
another button…
THUD!
"Ow!" says
Mister Wolf.
"That really hurt!"

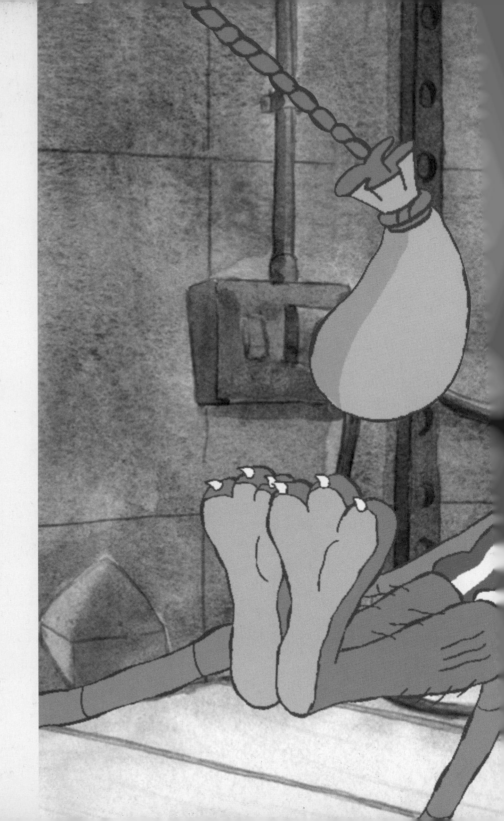

Next Preston goes to the science lab.
"What's in this jar?" says Preston.
"And what's this?" He pushes a button
and lights a flame. "Cool!" says Preston.

Preston starts messing around with a computer. Mister Wolf creeps up behind him. "What's that burning smell?" says Preston.

"**Aaaarrrggghhh!** My tail's on fire!" howls Mister Wolf, shooting through the roof.

crash!

"What was that?" says Preston, spinning around. "Strange! There's nobody there! Oh dear, look at the time. I've still got to choose a musical instrument.
I'd better get a move on!"

Back in the music room,
Preston looks around and
sees…a tuba!

   "Cool!" says Preston.
"That'll do nicely!"

Mister Wolf hears Preston locking the school door. "Okay!" says Mister Wolf. "This time, my little pork chop, there's no escape!"

Whee!

Guess where Mister Wolf lands?

Preston is trying out his tuba. Preston huffs and puffs, and huffs and puffs until…

P! Whoooooaahhh!

"Now that's what I call music!" says Preston.

"Sausages!" says Mister Wolf.

"I hate school!"

THE END